WORLDS APART

MICA JAY

The June Press

First published in 2005
Updated 2017

by The June Press Ltd

UK distributor
The June Press Ltd
PO Box 119, Totnes
Devon TQ9 7WA
Tel: 44(0)8456 120 175
Email: info@junepress.com
Web: www.junepress.com

ISBN 978-0-9927501-4-5

Acknowledgement

With thanks to VALERIE
ILLINGWORTH whose valuable
scientific observations
made this story more credible.

Valerie Illingworth edited the
Collins Dictionary of
Astronomy

A tribute to the visionary Tukuna tribes and courageous Uruba-Kaapor forest dwellers of the Brazilian Amazon.

"There is a third state of religious experience which belongs to all of them - and which I will call cosmic religious feeling."

ALBERT EINSTEIN

CONTENTS

INTRODUCTION

The universe came into being in an explosion some fourteen billion (thousand million) years ago. This is known as the Big Bang, and was the point at which time began. The universe was then infinitesimally small and infinitely dense! It has been expanding every since.

The primitive universe was extremely hot and turbulent but as it expanded it cooled. The first atoms – the lightest ones, mainly hydrogen and helium – could then be created. Gradually, after maybe hundreds of thousands of years, the expanding matter of the universe was able to form stars and the collections of stars called galaxies, all moving away from one another and each containing up to several hundred billion stars. The band of faint stars, the Milky Way, is part of the spiral galaxy in which the sun lies.

Stars have colours ranging from red, orange, yellow, white, to blue, which are dependent on their surface temperature and alter as the star reaches the end of its life. The sun is yellow; Sirius, the brightest (and almost the nearest) star in the sky, is white; Rigel, extremely distant, is the brightest star in the constellation Orion and is bluish white while Betelgeuse, the second brightest in Orion, is red.

But these stars do not last forever and over the age of the universe, heavier elements, including carbon, oxygen, neon and magnesium have been created in nuclear reactions in their centres. Stars like the sun have a lifetime of about ten billion years. As it dies the sun will expand into a red giant and ultimately collapse into a very small dense star known as a white dwarf while the brightest and most massive stars will shine for a few million years and then explode violently as supernovas.

Their outer regions, including newly formed elements, are blown off into space, mixing with interstellar cloud of gas and dust from which new stars are then formed. It was from this enriched matter that, much later, life began.

Any object remaining at the centre of a supernova collapses inwards becoming extremely dense and compact. It is then a neutron star and many of these have been observed in the remnants of supernovas in the form of pulsars. If the collapse cannot stop, however, the object becomes a black hole, a region of space in which the force of gravitation is so strong that nothing can escape, not even light. Any matter drawn into the black hole is utterly destroyed – yet its mass can increase.

There are probably super-massive black holes at the centres of many galaxies and it is even thought that at the turbulent beginning of the universe, mini black holes may have formed.

There are many bizarre objects in the universe and scientists continue to learn more about them using telescopes, spectrometers and other instruments. It is not possible to answer the question in scientific terms as to how the Big Bang came about. Or why. Perhaps man's quest to answer such questions led Albert Einstein, who described the force of gravity and the large-scale structure of the universe, to also talk of a "cosmic religious feeling".

Val Illingworth
Editor of Dictionaries of Astronomy published
by Collins and Macmillan

I

TAKE OFF

A deafening roar shattered the earth quiet and the sky burst into a mountain of fire.

The astronaut barely caught sight of the tops of trees and towns spread out like dice on bumpy tables when clouds blotted out his vision of earth.

It was T minus 28 hours on the controls as the powerful rocket propelled him into space. The rocket orbited the earth twice, three times at twenty seven thousand, eight hundred and fifty kilometres an hour before spinning on its elliptical orbit to the moon.

Freed like a foetus from his earth egg, the astronaut grew light like a bubble. He felt delirious – a foetus grown colossus astride his earth – and marvelled that fate had destined him, Fergus Faraday, an astronaut while other men lived such rooted and humdrum lives.

Secure in the knowledge that he knew everything necessary for his survival – how many kilograms of thrust from the rocket engine, how much fuel to burn per second, how many milliseconds to lapse between the different stages of manoeuvre and what their orbital rates should be – he could regard his fellow men with infinite superiority and marvel at the arrogance of earthmen who waged war continually to prove their infinitesimal differences.

What was 2,000 years of earth time or the fractional sum of an earthman's life when the universe could be 14 billion years old? And what was the sum of the universe itself when there were other suns and planets in our own galaxy over a hundred million light years across, and countless more in the billions of other galaxies?

He reflected on the trivialities of earthmen's lives while he, the ultimate celebrity, spun through space on his journey to the moon.

Not since Galileo had tossed stones off the leaning tower of Pisa had life reached such a turning point as this. He, Fergus Faraday, no less than a God in earthmen's eyes for his daring exploits in space, his enlightened theories on the moon and the solar system, and ponderous thoughts on anti-gravity and lunar mining, would be the inspiration for a new age of enlightenment.

Astronaut Faraday thought ecstatically of his starspattered destiny flowing with the speed of light and reflecting his image through the billion television screens of earthly homes.

....

Instead of earth, a vast primordial void
scattered with archipelagos of stars
and asteroids
where strands of nebulae trailed in the dusk
and spirals of light sailed slick as silver
on an endless sea
while earthman floated on and on
towards infinity......

II

THE FARADAY HOME

Many miles below, a small brick house caught the rays of the sun in its solar roof and channelled them along its glass walls to the home buried inside like a nest.

Protected from the harshness of the world outside by a barrage of trees, it inclined towards the sun at every available point, soaking up its warmth with huge radiators, while its occupants traced the sun's course like nomads from one day to the other and one season to the next.

Despite the comforts of her automated house, Mary Faraday felt like a prisoner. She abandoned the machines that whirred around her and sighed deeply as she clattered plates and cups through a bowl of soapy water, easing them through the bubbles that formed like frothy clouds over the top.

She imagined her husband piercing through the clouds on his way to the moon and dipped her fingers in the froth, drawing it from side to side so that it spilled over the edge of the bowl. The water beneath was grey and opaque.

She gazed instead through the steep glass roof where the arms of a cedar stretched against the sky. Once they planned to cut it down believing it blocked out the light before realising it formed a barrier against the gusty wind. She contemplated its deep green leaves and the sweep of the grass outside.

They had grown so apart, the woman in her solar home and the space celebrity that she hardly remembered the time when his universe centred round her. The magic of their past had been diminished by a new image of the world's first cosmic couple. It provided the ultimate escape for the narrow limits of earthman's world and its spiritual waste.

The name Faraday had spread throughout the world while Dr Faraday's face was displayed on billboards and posters promoting everything from toothpaste to cornflakes.

His acrobatic feats in space dominated the media, formed the subject of discussion groups and spawned movements for new theories on interstellar travel.

Words like "hibernation tank", "faster than light travel" and "wormhole" littered the dinner party scene, while invasions of well-wishers destroyed any last vestige of privacy the Faradays once had.

Once the intrusions gave meaning to Mrs Faraday's life. As the wife of a cosmic celebrity she could help to foster new ideals in their increasingly regimented world where new laws were announced almost daily by distant authorities who seemed to pass their days doing little else.

No wonder an astronaut could inspire such adoration as he spun about in the limitless freedom of space.

The crests of foam had vanished into the slops and Mrs Faraday emptied them down the drain.

At exactly seventeen hundred hours, James and Simon Faraday burst through the glass doors of their solar home in time for the televised news on the latest space transmission.

They could barely wait to see and hear the most recent exploits of their father, the cosmic explorer who touched the parameters of heaven and earth; who so dazzled the world with his daring feats that he was dubbed superman when he had barely left the earth a dozen times.

He would thrill them with tales of the birth and death of stars, of immense waterless seas on the moon with names like Serenity and Nectar, mysterious glowing craters lit by earthshine and multicoloured lights that showered like rainbows.
Names like Oceanus Procellarum and Lunar Carpathians would spin off their tongues with impressive facility as they calculated cosmic distances on computers stuffed inside their pockets like handkerchiefs, and their friends would regard them awestruck as if waiting for gamma rays to shoot from their eyes and envelop their bodies in an aura of gold.
In turn, they tuned in like radar to everyone's expectations of what they should be so it soon became clear they were as brilliant as their father.

....

III

CENTRE OF ATTRACTION

"There will be large areas of uniformly low pressure over the country" a voice announced.

"The main feature of the night will be fog followed by a lot of cloud and some drizzly rain."

The announcement ended with a blinding flash and a roar and Dr Faraday's smile spread like toothpaste over the screen.

"Well, hello everybody!", called the astronaut reassuringly, and he challenged his sons over the airwaves with a simple puzzle:

"What is two and a half times the speed of light multiplied by the square root of eight thousand seven hundred million?"

As they speedily calculated the answer, he manoeuvred his way through a hatch in the spacecraft without warning. Hanging precariously over the edge, he launched himself into space, floating and spinning like a slow motion top as the wire that attached him to his craft coiled around his feet and legs. Then he balanced a tiny camera on one gloved finger and loosened one of his boots so that it floated free like a white boat in the ether.

The men in the Space Control Centre sighed and tried to gauge the reaction of these latest hair-brained moves as they were signalled across the world. They swiftly calculated how the ruination of their precise schedules might nonetheless be salvaged by such wonderful publicity for a rocketing budget. A space age celebrity was a calculated risk.

To their relief and the disappointment of his fans, Astronaut Faraday floated back inside his craft and prepared to beam down his latest message to his wife:

"Well, Hi Mary", he ventured as she stood waiting and wondering over three hundred thousand kilometres away.

"Hi!" he called again, trying in vain to focus on their past which seemed too far away to have any meaning at all, when to his relief, the voice of the newsreader intervened:

"As you know, viewers, all those stars you see are moving around the centre of our galaxy at over two hundred kilometres a second. We can measure the velocity of a star along the line of sight towards us or away from us, using a spectrometer."

"Over two hundred kilometres a second!" wondered Mrs Faraday, imagining some eternal whirlpool sweeping away her husband.

The fact that he had entered a different orbit of time was beyond her comprehension. Something to do with the sun and the moon, she recalled, and the fact that the earth was turning continually while she remained stuck to it like a magnet.

"Matter, motion and light", she heard him say. "All objects fall towards a centre of attraction, the moon to the earth and the earth to the sun, as me to you.."

They were like the sun and the moon with their earth centre while the rest of the universe spread neatly around, sharing but never intruding in the space of their lives and its own immutable time.

"Red giants and white dwarfs, the dying stages of stars," the voice of the newscaster droned on.

"Number of kilometres of diameter one million three hundred and ninety two thousand", calculated Simon Faraday.

"Distance of the sun – one point six multiplied by ten to the minus five light years or eight light minutes", his brother James agreed.

For them time was eternal and in their universe nothing was impossible.

....

Astronaut Faraday sat like a hollow man drifting in water.

He slid his seat slowly along two tracks and lifted a bottle to his mouth. Very slowly he inclined the bottle and a cloud of bubbles seeped out and floated around his head.

Every movement he made in space and time was equal.

All the distances he covered left him unchanged.

Only infinity beckoned with its trail of glittering stars...

IV

THE MASONS

That evening the doorbell rang again. It was the regular weekly call of the Masons.

Mr Mason and Dr Faraday had been close friends since they met at school and later progressed to the same university. Mr Mason remembered Dr Faraday as a very skinny boy who set himself an interminable number of goals and achieved them all.

The solid healthy Mason finished his studies competently and settled for a solid government post where his technical training was rarely used and administrative skills he never realised were prized like gifts of Apollo. The athletic skills he once possessed were minimised to weekly rounds of golf followed by several more of beer.

Faraday, in his strive for perfection, had

meanwhile won a doctorate for his thesis on orbital rendezvous and spent his spare time reading books on high energy physics. He subsequently trained as a jet fighter test pilot after which he was selected to go on a solo mission to the moon.

His friend felt diminished when he heard of Faraday's latest glorious exploits and found himself listening and rarely contributing to any conversation they had on the rare occasions when they met. Without a challenge of his own, he was nonetheless greatly influenced by all that Faraday did and even followed him into marriage.

At this turning point he and his wife, a solid person like himself, began to confront life with a combination of resignation and peace that promised them a rosy future.

The Masons had three children. The eldest worked as assistant for a biogas company, the second followed a standard computer training course and the last was completing his last uneventful year at university.

Mr and Mrs Mason would once discuss their three children with the Faradays but since the Faraday children had begun to show such signs of genius, any attempts at comparison were clearly futile and they preferred to keep their thoughts about their own children to themselves.

With natural humility, they assumed they had little to communicate to the offspring they regarded nevertheless as unique and abandoned them to the various bodies described as educational.

Mrs Faraday, too, regarded her children with awe. What contribution had she made towards their brilliance when learning was so tedious to her with its association of rigid institutions and tests to confirm that those with natural aptitude were more able than those who found it impossible to channel their spirits into some sort of order?

As for Astronaut Faraday, he was always flying to the moon and thought little about it at all.

....

Simon and James Faraday remained glued to the television despite the arrival of the Masons.

"Lunar escape velocity – two point four kilometres per second", muttered James Faraday:

"Lunation – twenty nine point five three days." Simon Faraday nodded.

"...hydrogen, helium, neon, magnesium," continued James Faraday.

"Hum!..Yes", grunted Mr Mason.

They could catch a glimpse of the moon, now, squashed and dented like a rotten apple, Mr Mason thought. The three gazed at it fixedly.

....

V

ATOMS

Nearly three hundred and ninety thousand kilometres away, Astronaut Faraday studied the moon through the black void of the universe.

He could see vast circular plains and depressions sunk deep into the ground as if scooped out by some giant hand.

He did not believe that some superior being had created the universe, as perhaps his wife or the Masons might. "You know that is quite impossible," he heard himself say.

"The universe was created from atoms – billions and trillions of atoms that formed after a cataclysmic explosion and came together to produce the stars and galaxies, the sun and planets."

"I know you think that, Fergus," he heard his

wife reply:

"If I was you I would think exactly the same. But who put the atoms there in the first place and what are atoms anyway?"

"Atoms, Mary, are the smallest unit of an element that can take part in a chemical reaction and are made up of tiny particles of matter called electrons, protons and neutrons," he once explained.

"Atoms can lose or gain electrons to become charged ions – this happens in stars because of the high temperatures.

"The protons and neutrons together form the central nucleus of atoms," he would enthuse as he was an avid reader of physics.

"Energy is released when lighter nuclei are fused together to create other nuclei.

"Two hydrogen nuclei fuse to form a helium nucleus, and this is how stars like the sun create their energy and can be seen shining in the night sky.

"So I'm just a lump of atoms, dear!"

"Mary, we are all atoms bound together in all sorts of different molecules – proteins and fats and DNA.

"Tables and chairs are atoms. Atoms are everywhere!

"It was the Greek philosopher, Democritus,

who, years and years ago, described atoms as the indivisible units from which everything in the universe is built."

His wife would smile at the very idea of defining the universe in terms of atoms and atomic particles as if it could be explained by man's intellect alone.

Dr Faraday reflected how simple life must be for his wife who did not understand theories of relativity and gravity or particle physics.

He wondered about all those hours she spent scouring the media for trivialities which could, he admitted, be entertaining. But how useful were such trivia when you were flying through space?

But then, knowledge of the universe was hardly indispensable for running a home – though, there were times, he recalled, quickly eyeing the lights on the charts zig-zagging in front of him before permitting himself a sudden glimmer of realisation about his wife – there were times when she seemed to know about matters that should have been beyond her comprehension: the amount of energy in an electric current for example, and those quiet observations that were so truth shattering, those puzzles, tortuous even for him, that she so effortlessly solved. This was a conundrum the cosmic celebrity was unable to solve.

In fact Mary Faraday thought a great deal as she gazed up through the solar panelled roof and the sweep of cedar towards the sky.

It seemed that it was during moments like these that she most communicated with her husband, as if their thoughts were spinning together like a top, so the more scientific Dr Faraday's thoughts would appear, the more profound her musings on life.

What did time mean, she wondered, when thoughts could be transmitted much faster than light itself?

It was clear to Mary Faraday that there was a world of thought and perception that had none of the dimensions of her husband's universe.

....

VI

LIFE ON EARTH

Not far away Mrs Mason knew exactly how Mrs Faraday thought and felt, for she and her husband belonged to a religious cult spreading throughout the land.

While ancient churches had been abandoned in the frantic pursuit of pleasure, the cult of Janus provided the perfect antidote to their increasingly automated and regimented lives.

Every day they would perform certain rites to a special god who had two faces, one round and light like the sun, and the other, a heavy, brooding, omnipresent moon.

They understood that the enigmatic moon with its ever-changing forms, though a strangely obsolete power, was a force as necessary to their survival as the vibrant smouldering sun.

Mr Mason smiled at his wife as they prepared to celebrate this day twenty years ago when they first met during a protest march against the excessive regulations that ruled their daily lives.

From that day on, they demanded little more than the peace and quiet to enjoy what was left of them.

The moon transmissions were interrupted with the usual plethora of advertisements on computerised holidays – regular air transportation from home to airport and private helicopter service from airport to hotel and even to the nearest beach. Even so-called seaside hotels had stretched so far into the mainland that beaches were more and more inaccessible while those multi-storeyed edifices that fringed the teeming shores were so high and so wide that views of the sea were practically non-existent to those with limited income.

Every year the Masons would visit the same exclusive motel in southern Spain through the same super-efficient travel bodies for the same very reasonable price. The whole process was quite effortless and egalitarian and ensured the maximum of comfort and the minimum of effort.

As Mr Mason waited for his train on a draughty platform, crammed through silver doors and jostled his way to the centre of the city, he thought longingly of those balmy days when he merely had to rise in the morning and appear at regular intervals for meals, meeting pleasant people with the same interests – eating, drinking and enjoying the sun – and he thought how uncomplicated life could be.

Privileged as he was to have a home beyond the straggling anonymity of the suburbs, this journey took up almost half the day, and, as for those five daily hours of work – no more permitted under Euro regulation 11406000 – talking, reading, cups of tea, one or two decisions to be checked and re-checked, filing to be done, cups of tea, perhaps a beer or two before he made his way home – even these were bearable as long as he could take those frequent holidays.

As Mr Mason reflected longingly on sunshine and beaches, he glanced at the viewing screen on his watch and turned up the volume control:

"Sun is six thousand degrees Celsius at its surface rising to about fifteen million degrees at its centre", announced a voice as a vision of space loomed into view.

At this very moment Dr Faraday was landing on the moon.

....

VII

ON THE MOON

Astronaut Faraday prepared to land on the moon.

Above him loomed the earth, eighty times as bright as earthman saw the moon, and four times as large.

For some time he dabbled with the controls to extend the padded legs of the craft that would alight on the moon's dusty surface and ignite the descent engine.

Once he had been assisted by a small crew, but more sophisticated techniques had since been established by competing lunar entrepreneurs so that now he could travel alone, a fact which exalted his image even more in earthmen's eyes. Sure of his purpose and himself, he had adapted to the weightlessness of space like a fish in water.

Within one earth hour the craft had dropped some eighty thousand kilometres and was sweeping over the rugged highlands and the dark craters of the lunar surface.

Earthmen sat riveted to their viewing screens as their idol deftly landed his craft on the moon's surface. He checked his spacesuit with its life support system, jetpack and communication equipment, and lastly put on his helmet, lunar overshoes and thermally insulated gloves. Then he opened the hatch and stepped down on to the lunar surface.

The moon lay silent, a yellowish grey waste marked by inky black shadows. Experimental stations broke the lunarscape with a series of mirrors reflecting back narrow shafts of light like large wine glasses sipping the rays of the sun.

The astronaut opened his arms wide in his huge white suit and floated bulkily across the dusty surface with the aid of his jetpack. The whole world would be watching him, as always on his lunar expeditions.

"My lunar kingdom", he thought proudly, momentarily forgetting his role as a pioneer space scientist in the euphoria of the moment. He felt indeed like a king-god in this immense universe of countless billions of stars.

He leaned over and prodded the specks of dust

with his lunar probe. They were soft and flaky like the cinders of a fire. He reflected how the tread of his lunar overshoe would remain for another five hundred thousand years unless erased by some falling micrometeorites.

As he floated across the moon, the astronaut marvelled that for so many millions of years the sun and the moon had performed their ritual dance with earth to produce creatures like himself.

And yet, he reflected soberly, earthman's infinitesimal analysis of life had reduced him to just a heap of subatomic particles more meagre than the very specks of dust beneath him.

Momentarily humbled by this glimpse of his earthly limitations, the astronaut concentrated on the mission at hand and stopped to probe between clumps of black basaltic paste and molten rock that glowed like phosphorus.

None of the moon probings had so far revealed any evidence of its origin or how it had settled into its orbit around the earth as earth's only natural satellite.

His mission to investigate its source would include prospecting those very same minerals that may have solidified when the moon was formed or fused from the debris of outer space. He would also need to check data from craters to assess the possibility of a cataclysmic bombardment of the moon and early earth by meteorites some four billion years ago.

Wealthy speculators had planned moon trips for tourists and he feared his scientific experiments might be abandoned before they had even borne fruit in the mad pursuit of earthly pleasures.

He made his way to a lunar vehicle to transport him to the nearest experimental station. Here he could analyse the latest data from surface instruments, noting heat flow, gravity, magnetism, moonquakes and meteorite impacts.

With his latest collection of ancient lunar rocks, including porous basalt, breccia and billion year old troctolites, the astronaut returned to his spacecraft, stopping to peer at some crystalline formation that resembled green pearls before he prepared his ascent.

The spacecraft rose above the pockmarked face of the moon and he could see below him craters gouged out by meteorites sunk into its sterile waste.

As he sat behind the controls, something flashed through the earthman's brain.

"Forms of electromagnetic wave travelling at the speed of light", he noted and swayed a little.

"Viridian, lime the palest shoots of....", he felt

quite dizzy.

The lunar crust spread before him like a surrealist dream and sank deep into the black night sky.

....

VIII

LIVE ON TV

Mrs Faraday and her two sons and Mr and Mrs Mason settled down to their meal as the interminable television advertisements came to an end and the moon transmissions resumed.

They could see Astronaut Faraday floating over the lunar surface with the aid of his jetpack. He looked like a balloon in his thick white thermal suit. The picture was hazy but they could make out clumps of rock and deep rifts sunk into the moon's crust.

Of course this was not the first time they had seen him land on the moon. His visits were frequent and always highlighted by learned scientific discussions on the origin of the moon and the possibility of a giant telescope on its far side, as well as the effects of loss of gravity on his heart and other muscles which grew a little smaller, and his bones which grew a little longer each time he returned to earth so he was just a little taller than before.

They could see him now swaying slightly and climbing into a large four-wheeled truck which the announcer explained was propelled by the rays of the sun.

....

Mrs Faraday served her guests mechanically. She had a vague feeling of unease, the culmination of a day's fruitless reminiscences, and wished that the transmission was over.

After a number of years of marriage, she and her husband had fitted so minutely into the fabric of each other's lives that they could almost have become one person.

She had even been afraid to leave her home without the reassurance of her husband beside her. But this attachment floundered as Dr Faraday immersed himself more and more in his scientific activities and spent less and less time at home.

She saw his reserve as a reflection of her own

inadequacy and searched tortuously within herself for the answer. Then it became clear – the early morning nine kilometre jogging, the fanatical accumulation of scientific data and long spells of meditation – that Dr Faraday, not content with his above-average strength and athleticism, was striving to create another image of himself, a superior being unequalled in the history of the world.

"So you think Spain will be fine?"

Mr Mason's question interrupted Mrs Faraday's thoughts.

"How can stars disappear?" interrupted Simon Faraday.

"Yes, Spain's fine," sighed Mrs Mason as her hostess served more helpings of food even though no one had asked for any.

"A really massive star," explained James Faraday "will reach the end of its life when it has run out of nuclear fuel and then it will explode – and what remains of the star may then collapse inwards so completely that it becomes a black hole.

"A black hole is a region of space in which the force of gravitation is so strong that nothing, not even light, can escape, and the force of gravity is so extreme that it completely distorts the passage of time so time runs slower and slower and at its very centre the laws of physics go quite haywire."

Mr and Mrs Mason continued their meal while Simon Faraday and his mother stared at the screen.

"There are probably super-massive black holes at the centres of many galaxies," explained James Faraday.

"Some scientists even believe that mini black holes may have formed when the universe began but these have probably all disappeared by now...."

James Faraday's words were sliced abruptly by a queer ringing sound and a light flashed across the television screen which became as black as the night sky.

No further sound was emitted from the television. Not a sound was uttered in the Faraday home. The little party sat transfixed as Mrs Faraday rose to clear the dishes.

....

As minutes ticked by in the Faraday home,
oceans of time streamed across the universe
threaded amongst strands of primordial gas
and nebulae encrusted with stars.
Atoms linked into galaxies and planets spun
slowly around their suns.
In the cosmos a silhouette slid along the
rays of a shadow clock bearing the world
on its shoulder as a colossus might
amongst a tiny breed of men
and in the breathing space between the planets
a fragment of life exploded in the dusk
and vanished...

IX

AFTERMATH

Time had come to a standstill in the Faraday home. Days lost their routine and sequence, and nights, instead of shadowing their pattern, distorted them into grotesque and tortuous shapes. Only the old cedar seemed as solid as ever as it gathered up the day's light for its imperceptible growth and sank into each night like a huge drop of sedative in a vessel of water.

Mary Faraday moved as an automaton in and out of rooms, ineffectually puffing up huge cushions and dusting shelves and tables several times a day. Even trips to the nearest stores had become an ordeal as she was continually subjected to curious, sympathetic or just penetrating stares.

But the dullness of the day was an antidote to

the night's torments and the dream that would recur over and over again.

She would see a figure, floating like a balloon in space. The figure would stare down at her with hollow eyes and call out with a mocking voice that sounded like that of her husband:

"Atoms. Atoms are everywhere!"

"We are all atoms – tables and chairs, buildings and stars... Atoms are the smallest unit of an element that can take part in a chemical reaction and are made up of tiny particles of matter called electrons, protons and neutrons."

"It was the Greek philosopher, Democritus, who, years and years ago, described atoms as the indivisible units from which everything in the universe was built."

....

Fewer people came to visit the Faraday home, while she, now a single woman, made odd numbers at dinner tables and was rarely invited out. Even visits from the Masons became more and more infrequent.

"Mr Mason is working late," his wife would say.

"He is launching a new project on space tourism. The usual holiday spots are so overcrowded and even the countryside has become a vast theme park."

Only Mrs Mason would occasionally call and discuss the latest progress of her children. The eldest, Michael, was training to be a lawyer. He was going to specialise in patents, as inventions were increasing by the million, she disclosed. And then there was Elaine – such imagination! – planning to follow an electronic art course; while Christopher, indecisive, but a choice is difficult when you are accomplished in so many different ways, had changed his mind so many times. Perhaps a career in the growth area of gambling syndication would prove prosperous? What did Mrs Faraday think? Did she know that Christopher played the guitar in the regional music assembly? They were called "The Mystics".

Simon Faraday was becoming known as a failure. His concentration would lapse. He would doodle on bits of paper. He no longer troubled to try and solve problems but simply abandoned them if they appeared difficult.

He would stare out of windows and up at the sky and into space. Nothing pleased him more than the end of the day and he would try to draw it nearer by rising later and later so that there were fewer hours to trouble him.

He picked at his food and approached every event as if it was part of an obstacle race. Being close to his mother, he mirrored her despair and the days of futility flowed endlessly on. He feared he would never more impress his friends and they, in turn, felt sorry for him. Fancy basking in his father's glory for so long!

For James Faraday life was constantly renewing and renewable. He viewed it as a scientific puzzle. Nothing was impossible and he accepted nothing unless he personally had proven its worth.

Already he had exhausted the reading matter at his university and had to rely instead on his own resources and calculations. His insatiable curiosity and open mind redressed the balance of the Faraday spirit which swung precariously near to resignation.

Whereas his brother saw himself doomed in the eyes of his friends, James never paused to consider their opinion. He judged everything according to its own merits and was thereby judged on his own estimation of himself.

The Faraday house was silent. James Faraday

slept like a log beside his astronomy books and magazines, surrounded by a radio, television, telescope and computer.

He had charted an astronomical map above his bed and made some calculations on radio galaxies before falling asleep. For hours he had been trying to explain the effects of communication breakdown to his mother but she did not appear to be listening and he had finally abandoned his efforts exhausted.

Across the corridor, Simon Faraday tossed and turned like a ship in a storm. He saw phantoms shaped like white balloons and snow flakes streaming across mountains.

The snowflakes were changing into hailstones and then into huge rocks that cascaded through the sky as if hurled by an enraged giant, while a small world spun and spun so fast it whirled off its axis and reeled giddily into space.

On and on sped the world, choking up its rivers and mountains and burying its little people in the sky, all the time growing smaller and smaller until it resembled a tiny marble, veined with blue and green.

Simon Faraday spun giddily with the blue and green marble, his legs and arms flailing as it gathered speed and sucked him along on a mysterious trail.

The marble began to wail like a siren, louder and louder as it streaked along, now growing larger and larger until it grew back into a world and the blue and green veins changed into rivers and forests. As it grew, the world began to scream until Simon Faraday could bear no more. Desperately he struggled to be free before the world lay before him, crushed in a giant hand.

Mrs Faraday had swallowed three small green pills to make her sleep.

She could see a bubble floating in a vessel of water. The bubble grew and grew until the vessel shrunk to a speck. As it grew, it spun away from the vessel leaving long strands of ribbon flowing behind.

The strands of ribbon floated and waved and the bubble grew so big it burst into a myriad colours. The colours floated off along the strands of ribbon and when Mrs Faraday woke, the birds told her it was dawn.

....

The sun dipped towards the western horizon
in a shimmering arc of colours,
each stretching its luminous band across
the irridescence like a cluster of priceless jewels
and separating sharply as if to diminish
its own imperious splendour.
Yellow glittered like gold as it soaked up the
light waves and filtered through the sky.
Then a flame of crimson burnished brown
followed by green sparkling emeralds,
and in its trail, an indigo sky and purple sea.
Very slowly the fiery incandescence faded
leaving only a ring of shining blue
like a new earth....

X

IN THE FOREST

The late sun shone through a lining of clouds revealing a narrow channel of water winding its way through deep forest. Flashes of blue skirted the green fringe while, sunk into the shadows of the trees, lay thick carpets of wet leaves.

Suddenly the peace of the forest was disturbed by a strange metal object attached to a parachute which descended from the sky like a huge teardrop and plunged towards the river. As it touched the water, the parachute swept downstream leaving the module to drift towards the shore where it was caught in a tangle of bushes. The heavy foliage echoed with sudden screeches and shrills and birds flapped their way wildly up into the branches. Then there was silence.

Further along the blue channel a rooster crowed the arrival of dawn and a sweet musky odour wafted around a forest sanctuary.

A woman climbed down from a house of bamboo and quaria palm which rose on stilts by the riverbank and strolled through a grove of breadfruit and papaya to a small shelter. Gathering up some manioc roots in her arms she returned to the house and called out:

"Paolo!"

A slight man emerged from the house dressed in a pair of shorts. He climbed down to a nearby canoe, untied the mooring rope and clambered inside.

"I'm off fishing, Elena! Adeus!" he called back and gently guided the boat downstream.

The fisherman's boat drifted for some time past skeletal trees with twisted barks devoured by termites and hung with liana or nests of egrets. Then he paused to tie his boat to an overhanging branch and tossed a fishing net into the river.

For some time he sat there quietly fishing beneath a red bromelia while swallows swooped across the water and a woodpecker chopped into one of the hollow barks with its bill.

Paolo looked at the sun. It was three hours after sunrise. He sat patiently watching the trees reflected in the water. The water lay still, like glass, so it was impossible to tell which was water and which sky.

A flight of toucans swept across the surface and he listened to the chirpings and shrills around him and thought how tomorrow he would hunt pigs or tapir now there was less sign of rain.

Paolo knew every whisper in his small corner of the world, every flower, every tree and every turn of the tide that swept up from the sea with the changing seasons.

As he fished, he heard a sound through the trees and he turned warily as the toucans swept with alarm through the still air and even the woodpecker stopped its steady tap tap against the hollow tree.

It wasn't the usual crash of a falling branch, the cry of a jaguar in a trap, or the sound of a tapir hunting for food or a monkey swinging from tree to tree. The sound came again, a heavy tramping sound like footsteps on a carpet of leaves. He sat in his small dug-out canoe and carefully studied the trees.

As Paolo looked around him, a branch of one of the trees was slowly folded aside and an apparition met his eyes that he had never encountered in all the years in which he had glided through his tranquil, if mysterious world.

There, on the opposite bank of the river, was a tall stooped figure, his face as pale as bleached wood and his body covered in a thick white material with what appeared to be a network of tubes supporting his arms.

For some time the figure stood motionless, staring right through Paolo as the fisherman sat dumbfounded in his tiny boat. Then the strange man shouted and waved his arms and seemed to gaze up at the sky.

The fisherman watched the white man, now gazing at his own reflection as if expecting it to fade away, and the white man looked at the fisherman sitting so peacefully in his boat full of fish and watched a green leaf float lightly on to the water, as if he had never seen such a thing before. They were like two beings from two different worlds.

Paolo looked up at the sun once more. It was exactly three hours before sunset. Soon night would fall like a black cloud. He took one last glance at the apparition and paddled off in his canoe.

. . . .

XI

THE VISION

Long after darkness had fallen, Paolo's wife, Elena, worked the manioc machine, stuffing the bulky roots into it and watching the fine grains fall into the basin below, while her husband strung up hammocks across the beams of the house, lit up some kerosene lamps and kindled a log fire.

Great pools of diamonds had filled the night sky and shone through the turmoil of frothy clouds that had left the air fresh and cool under its forest canopy.

As the flames of the fire grew brighter, the family gathered to cook the basketful of fish that Paolo had brought back for their meal, and sat together under the shimmering sky listening to the wails and cries of the forest and the sound of the water lapping against the riverbank.

As they sat there, Paolo described how the river had appeared as still as glass and how the next day he would hunt tapir or pigs as there would be no rain. Before his children slept he told the story of Light, passed down to them by their ancestors – how, before heaven and earth appeared, everything was covered in darkness while the wind puffed and blew and slowly filled the night until an egg was formed. This egg, said Paolo, split into two halves. The top half formed a sky and the lower half an earth and out of the egg came light.

Then he told them: "Today I learnt how our world was created – the earth, the river, the animals and plants – for today I saw our God!"

....

From that day on Paolo's fame spread throughout the forest world and neighbouring families would come to talk about the strange white God.

Paolo said he came from a miracle jungle city filled with white man's luxuries, little machines that gave out sound, as if thousands of tiny men were talking inside, and magic lights that lit up the night like little moons.

Some said his home was made from glass and could be found deep in the forest while others were sure it lay at the other end of the river. A few even said he was really darker-skinned like they were but painted himself with white juice from some herb in order to wander disguised through his world.

Paolo explained how, long, long ago, when people were good, everyone could visit this God at his home but that everyone had become so greedy there was no hope for the future and he preferred to remain alone. But, he said, he wasn't sure whether God had visited them as a warning or to reassure them that everything was all right. He described how he had stood there as if transfixed.

"So still," described Paolo, "and dressed in white with such strange things attached to his body, like wings, that he must surely have come down from the sky."

"Did he say anything?" his family asked excitedly:

"What words did he speak?"

Paolo had to admit he wasn't sure which language the white god had spoken:

"It could have been a mixture of the languages

of all our different tribes", he said at last.

Then he explained:

"Man first appeared in the world when heaven and earth were united. But the more men there were, the less they were able to understand each other.

"So God piled up huge mounds of earth, higher and higher, until this mountain reached the sky, in order that men could share their problems with those in heaven and those in heaven could always give them advice.

"Our God carefully organised the men to carry out his plan and prepared two succulent fish which he divided up between them so that all would have an equal share of food.

"But his careful plans were ruined by one greedy man who snatched both fish when nobody was looking and ate them all himself.

"At that very moment a spell fell over the people. Each person shouted different words with different sounds and no-one could make himself understood, and, as they all shouted, the great mountain of earth they worked so hard to build slowly crumbled around them so that they were all tossed into different parts of the world.

"And since, from that time, it became impossible for men to understand each other, it was equally impossible to try to unite heaven and earth," Paolo concluded: "which is why I could not understand what the white God said. He just shouted and waved his arms like a terrible warning and then stood still, so still the water seemed to flow past him like a dream."

"Are you sure?" his brother asked him one day, "that you weren't dreaming yourself?" But Paolo had seen his God as clearly as he saw the changing of the seasons and the river flowing through the forest.

....

XII

THE GOLD PROSPECTOR

The white figure watched the fisherman paddle off in his canoe, dazed as if he had seen a vision. Why didn't the fisherman talk to him? Had he grown wings? Was he dreaming? Where had he been and why was he here? What was this water doing here and how did these trees appear and why was he wearing this strange plastic suit? Where, indeed, were his wife and family or had he ever had a wife and family?

He stared at the water confused and miserable. He did not know who or what he was but his body felt excessively weak and heavy and he could hardly walk or even lift his arms, added to which he was finding it increasingly difficult to focus his gaze on anything at all. He thought again of the fisherman and his boat full of fish and tried to pull himself up to his full height, gazing up at the sky, puzzled.

Night had fallen suddenly and the trees and the water were shrouded in darkness. The sky began to fill with stars flickering and shimmering like diamonds, and through the diamonds, the moon appeared, full and round like a beautiful golden sphere.

He stretched out and touched his clothing and the leaves of the trees around him, still damp with rain. Then he leaned over and trailed his fingers in the water until he could see rivulets form and swell around the edge of the sphere of gold before falling asleep on a carpet of leaves.

When he awoke he saw the moon had turned into bright sunshine and the river appeared green and still as glass while an endless trail of ants was crawling across him like a determined army on its way to war. Still confused and too weak to complete the task of removing his cumbersome suit, he left one of his arms and legs covered by a knitted nylon undergarment and the rest of his body adorned with a network of plastic tubing and groped at a battered backpack beside him.

He struggled to shout but his voice was drowned by the noisy shrieks and shrills of the forest. He stared helplessly at the river and watched in alarm as the ants continued their frantic leaf cutting trail to farm the fungus for their nests.

Once more he tried to stand but stumbled weakly and fell back on to a carpet of rotting leaves. Was the white God destined to be swallowed up in this strange world of fungus and tiny ants?

He lay delirious. He could see meters and charts zig zagging crazily. A hand moved slowly...viridian, emerald...the hand swivelled... daffodil leaves.. green glass....

Slowly the water dribbled down the throat of the prostrate figure lying limp on the pile of dead leaves. The crystal clear water felt cool and refreshing as it coursed through his veins. A thin man was lifting up his head and thrusting a flask into his mouth.

"Frozen leaves," he muttered, gulping it down as the thin man stared at him wide-eyed.

"Looks like he's dropped down from the sky!" exclaimed the thin man to himself.

He began to heave the figure away from the crawling ants on to a small motor boat moored nearby, picked up the backpack that lay alongside him and clambered inside before pushing away from the bank with a long oar.

The two men drifted off down the river beneath trees dripping with ivy and assorted creepers and twisted barks, hung with lianas, that rose eerily out of the water.

The sick man felt himself floating and swirling in and out of the trees and wondered if he was still dreaming. Occasionally something would tug at the boat and they would stop abruptly before drifting on with a jerk.

He watched the small slight figure in faded blue jeans bailing out water from the middle of a boat with a tin bowl before steering it along the banks of what had now turned into a noisy rushing river and starting the motor.

The thin man in turn glanced down at his strange companion in his extraordinary tattered white clothing and huge boots and leant over to peer curiously at the battered pack at his side. At one point he tried to force the bag open with his foot while its owner lay lifeless, his eyes closed as if dead.

Unable to restrain his curiosity any longer, he steered the boat towards the shore and moored it while he searched in his pocket for a small penknife which he used to prize open the bag.

Nothing could have prepared him for the weird assortment of tiny mechanisms and radio equipment that met his eyes. Not even a knife or a piece of string – hardly the needs of a traveller in equatorial forest!

Then he caught sight of a transparent bag filled with specimens of rock. Now this was much more interesting. Filled with excitement, he tore it open and stared for some time at the pieces of rock. Then he took out a small book from his pocket that he always carried with him on his journeys and flicked back and forth through the pages. All his life he had studied rocks and minerals, from the time he left Idaho and went to Colorado to hunt deer and elk before moving to Australia and New Guinea.

As a prospector he had gone in search of precious metals and that noblest one of all, gold, often starving and more often lonely and always with the help of his little pocket book on minerals. But never had he seen such an odd combination of igneous and crystalline rock with molten lava.

"Must have travelled to the moon!" He grinned at the prostrate man. Perhaps he was a geologist?

....

The sick man smiled weakly.
The Universe was expanding.
Wavelengths were passing through matter.
Isaac Newton was tossing apples through
black holes.
The apples were bobbing on mercury and
flashing like kilowatt bulbs
and little people spun and vanished
like ground to earth missiles...

XIII

SURVIVAL

The prospector was finding it more and more difficult to manoeuvre his boat. Huge landslides had swept tree barks and stumps into the river and they lay damming up the flow of the current while further upstream a barrage of stones diverted its course along a series of whirlpools.

As water began to leak slowly through the hull, his passenger stared anxiously over the sides. The trees had begun to cast shadows on the water and the noisy river had trickled into a stream where water bubbled over stones covered in moss and fern and seeped under lichen deep inside the forest.

The prospector glanced at a large gold watch clamped to his sinewy wrist and noted the time – late afternoon. Darkness would fall suddenly and the leak in the boat was increasing by the minute.

He stopped the motor and let the boat drift towards a sandy inlet where lianas looped amongst sentinels of bamboo – an ideal spot to rest.

He dragged the boat on to the beach, spread out a sheet of tarpaulin over the sand and heaved his sick companion on to it.

Leaving him to listen to the shrills and hisses of the forest, he went to search for seed pods from a huge kapok tree, drew out some dry tree cotton, tucked it into the hollow of a stick which he thrust into the ground and drew a thong of vine back and forth over the stick as the late sun beat down on to the sand.

But the sun's rays were growing gradually weaker and he abandoned the stick and the vine and searched instead for a piece of dry wood.

Carefully he grated the wood with his penknife, scooped out its pithy centre to make a groove, and scraped the end of the stick up and down inside the groove faster and faster until the wood dust flickered and burst into flames.

As the prospector fed the flames with twigs and leaves, the sick man lay inanimate, gazing at the strange wiry saviour who had appeared so suddenly from the blue with his book of minerals.

Now the prospector was prodding one of the

bamboo trees and cutting one of the rings of its trunk with his sheath knife.

For some time he chopped away at the bamboo trunk until he had cut away a slice the size of a dish, which he set near the fire. Then he sliced one of the leaf stalks of a palm, wound it on to a rod with liana, and grooved the rod into the sand so that the line hung loosely in the water.

He did not have to wait long before retrieving his first catch of the day, a sullen looking hatchet fish which was to form part of their evening meal.

It seemed that every fibre or plant he touched would be transformed into a vehicle for survival. His small rucksack was stuffed with oddments – gadgets, powdered food, bits of wire, a magnet, water bottles and all the paraphernalia of those for whom home can be anywhere.

Having prepared the fish, the prospector emptied his bag on to the sand, threw the fish into a tin can with some peeled bananas and cooked them over the fire.

His companion watched him carefully. He recalled small dehydrated packages of flakes or pineapple cubes and thought vaguely of a gun which injected water into his food. Was it a dream?

The two men feasted on the fish and bananas silently watching the sun set over forest. The prospector had now filled the tin pot with water which he boiled over the embers of the fire, adding coffee, the juice of a lemon, a spoonful of sugar and two more of rum.

His companion felt himself falling, falling down towards the river as a hot drink of coffee and rum slid down his throat. Then darkness fell and the forest orchestra was left to play its night-time symphony of haunting shrieks and shrills.

....

XIV

A RIVER JOURNEY

Hot sun shone through the banana leaves and dappled the sand around the tarpaulin while the stream bubbled cheerily alongside.

"I thought you'd never wake up!" cried the prospector. "I've been trying to figure out your bits of stone but I reckon they must've fallen from another planet. What are you going to do with them?"

"I don't know if they are mine," his companion said slowly.

"But they must be yours. They were in your bag," insisted the prospector. "Everything that's in my bag is mine."

He saw that the man had regained some strength and wondered if he had escaped from a lunatic asylum. Who else would go wandering through the forest with such strange equipment and a suit with tubes running round the back?

Thanks to the nourishment he had been given, the pure air of the forest and the peace of his surroundings, the sick man was slowly beginning to recover.

"The temperature on the protective heat shield must have been about three thousand degrees," he suddenly leaned forward and muttered, "the heat shield burnt away and the gases from the combustion products ionised, causing the communications blackout!" he whispered.

"Yep," the other nodded, "I'd black out too in a temperature of three thousand degrees!"

The prospector stood up and yawned: "We'll have to do something about that boat or we'll jus' sink to the bottom of the river!"

He began to hum in a hoarse, croaky voice as he pulled the boat further up the beach and peered at the wooden hull.

"Hum, hum teedum."

The sick man gazed up at the sky for some time with the same puzzled look that the fisherman saw when he paddled away in his canoe. Then he fell back weakly on to the tarpaulin leaving the prospector to repair the leaking hull with a piece of torn shirt and gum from a nearby vine.

Once dried by the heat of the sun, the newlyrepaired boat pulled away from the narrow inlet with the two men aboard, one steering to avoid unexpected rocks and tangled ivy while the other stared over the prow with a mixture of helplessness and disdain. Neither spoke, though the steersman hummed occasionally in a coarse tuneless voice as the boat chugged alongside the banks of the river.

The man at the prow looked carefully at the blue water and the trees as if trying to piece them together like a jigsaw puzzle. His body felt heavy and cumbersome as though tied to his surroundings by one of the lianas that curled around the trees.

The days and nights seemed to have grown longer and his mind had filled with images and colours that jostled and re-arranged like pieces of glass in a kaleidoscope. He stared across the undulating patterns of green of the riverbanks.

The current was flowing swiftly now, forcing the boat to twist and turn as the prospector steered it over rapids and amongst watery archipelagoes, forever humming tuneless songs in his croaky voice. Occasionally he would glance up at the sky to see if there would be rain or stared dolefully across at the odd tattered man in white who could have led him to some paradise of gold instead of rambling on like someone from outer space and tempting him with weird pieces of rock.

In the distance the prospector could just see the roofs of a mission centre in a nearby village. He stopped humming for a while to concentrate on steering the boat towards it, calling out to his sick companion to prepare for their arrival in the village.

But his companion, far from being pleased at the prospect of more human company, became anxious and fearful. If the fisherman had vanished at the very sight of him and the prospector found him so ridiculous, how would he be greeted by a whole community of people in this remote forest world?

As their motorboat stopped chugging and drifted towards the shore, a group of children appeared on the river bank and youths playing football in a grassy square paused briefly to stare before continuing their game.

The prospector slung the two packs on his back and helped his companion out of the boat as the children giggled and pointed. The man was stooped and seemed to have difficulty walking. He must have come from the hospital in the forest which was full of mad people.

The two men made their way slowly through

the village followed by the children and stopped outside a small brick house where the prospector tapped impatiently on the door.

Moments later it was opened by a dark-skinned woman, her hair tied back with a crimson scarf.

"Luiza!"

"Ah! Meu amigo!" the woman cried out delightedly and went to embrace the prospector. Then her gaze fell on the man in white, standing awkwardly nearby and her expression shifted from amazement to curiosity. Clearly this was someone in need of great care! She smiled at him graciously and offered him her arm to escort him inside. Nothing at that moment could have brought the stranger so swiftly back to earth.

Encouraged by the warmth and companionship of the woman, Luiza, with whom he managed to communicate in simple sign language, and the comfort of her clean and orderly home, the stranger was regaining his memory.

Though still very weak and finding it difficult to coordinate his movements, he thought again of the incident of the burning heatshield that came to him as he was lying by the river and had deduced that radio waves were unable to pass through ionised clouds. But what he could not explain was how he found himself lapsing into some universal dream-like state in which his mind plunged to unfathomable depths of nightmare and exaltation.

Was this some enchantment of his new forest world or the result of a cosmic experience from which even his heatshield could not protect him?

From the perspective of everyday life it was the small oddities that brought him relief – repeating the words "far away" had spun his thoughts back to "Faraday", though he did not remember that this name brought him fame and fortune.

The man who had always prided himself on achieving the impossible with his superb logic and tenacity was now floundering in uncertainty. Identity seemed fragile and precarious. Unknown in this distant corner of the world, he would have to search for it all over again.

Money, too, was a problem. Where could he find money to take him where he needed to go? And where should he go? He could hardly depend on the prospector who lived from day to day on whatever life had to offer him.

Seated in a comfortable chair in Luiza's home, he would look at his white bulky suit and let his mind take him to some corner of the universe in which a violent struggle was taking place of which he was clearly still a part.

....

XV

OFFICIALDOM

The prospector concluded that his companion must be harmless since children and dogs appeared unafraid in his presence and he was now able to utter clear, if unintelligible words.

The only solution to his predicament, he explained to him, was to consult a public official who would know exactly what to do. The nearest official was in the local health department, a large building on the other side of the village which stood next to an old wooden trolleybus painted with cartoons.

The two men made their way across the square, watched by an elderly couple seated beneath a jacaranda tree, who glanced briefly in their direction before continuing their conversation. The door of the local health department had been left ajar to catch the late afternoon breeze and the two men ventured inside.

In the middle of the room, seated by a desk, was a weary-looking man in an open-necked shirt and grey trousers. One of his shoes lay furled near the edge of the desk while the other slipped slowly off his other foot as his head lolled dangerously near a bottle of whisky.

The top of the desk was strewn with papers, though the room was otherwise bare save for an old record player and a series of photographs of the country's most renowned sights, with the same man beaming from each foreground.

"Hey, Alberto!" called the gold prospector.

"I have a friend for you!"

Alberto shook himself out of his slumber and stared over at the two men, blinking a couple of times to be sure that what he saw was quite real. One didn't often see a man in a torn white plastic suit with tubes running round his body and huge white boots. Perhaps the man was a little mad?

Alberto had met mad people before. There were a few at the university in the next town where he was professor. The Director was one of them. He, Alberto, knew the Director was stealing money from the university funds.

And then there was the affair at the farm where he lived with his mother and nephew. What had happened to all those chickens that vanished one night? He suspected his cousin, Miguel, who had been thrown out of the army. Miguel was known to take a mysterious drug.

"Well, what do you want?" he asked the men in broken English. He knew the gold prospector well. He was often in the village with that woman, Luiza, or searching for mining engineers in the local bar.

"I need your help," said the stranger. "I have to return to my country."

"Did you have an accident?" Alberto inquired. The man didn't look as though he came from anywhere except perhaps the moon!

"I remember being on some scientific mission," he heard him say, "but something happened to my controls".

"Yes, yes," Alberto replied impatiently. The whisky had given him a headache. He didn't have much control himself.

"Do you know to which country you belong?"

"Europe" he heard.

Yes, that was a possibility. He dialled a number, tapping his head in an agitated manner while the gold prospector wandered out into the sunshine leaving clouds of smoke from a cigarette dangling from his mouth.

Alberto was in a quandary. He was unable to

make contact with his friend in the travel department who was no doubt sleeping after a late lunch and here he was stuck with a madman. He seemed quite harmless but then he couldn't be sure.

He dialled the police before realizing that that was no solution. Only last week the chief of police had quarrelled with the governor of the state and released all the prisoners from his jail.

He turned to the new arrival: "Do you have identity papers?"

"I have no papers. I didn't need any," the stranger explained.

Did not need any papers! Everybody needed papers. How else could a person be identified as a person?

"What did you do on your mission?" he asked suspiciously.

"Collect rocks, assess the effect of weightlessness," the stranger seemed to be regaining his memory, "check out the earth-moon Lagrangian points".

"Where did you go?" he interrupted, his eyes as round as saucers:

"The moon?"

He shook his head impatiently. The man was obviously mad and should be locked up.

Alberto shuffled back into his shoes, pushed

some papers around his desk so that several fell on to the floor and beckoned him through a side door.

No venture into space had left Dr Faraday so helpless as his dealings with the government health official whose mind was as closed as the door he banged behind him, and locked securely, before returning to his afternoon slumber and bottle of whisky.

Not even the vast emptiness of space had left him feeling so abandoned as in the room with its one barred window which now imprisoned him and he wondered again how it was that a man who held the earth in his sway as he manoeuvred round the moon could be so humiliated.

. . . .

XVI

REFLECTION

It took weeks for Faraday to penetrate the layers of officialdom of the forest world, for not one official was very sure what the others did.

Alberto would make frantic calls to various people who would later appear on the brightly coloured wooden bus. He would talk for hours with his new arrivals, tapping his head in an agitated manner. Later he would pour them whisky as they listened to ballads on his record player.

At some stage they would open the door of the room in which Faraday sat and stare at him with curiosity or amusement, or very occasionally, a little sympathy.

Then nothing would happen for days and Faraday would try to reason with Alberto and ask him what he was doing to help. But since he himself remembered so little, any progress was slow. Only the woman Luiza would visit him regularly with food and drink and a reassuring smile.

In his solitary state, Faraday became more and more meditative. He had always been in such a hurry to finish one event and move on to the others that the days and weeks had rushed past leaving him barely time to reflect on what he was doing.

Even on a mission there were always the routine tasks, performing experiments, checking water absorption devices to keep humidity under control, reconverting packages of food with his water injection gun and other routine processes involved in space survival while the silence of space would be drowned by the noise of ground communicators humming through his earphones or the thump of the spacecraft thrusters as he steered his way out of orbit at a speed of forty thousand, three hundred and twenty kilometres an hour.

Now, here he was seated in this jungle prison, tied to the earth like an umbilical cord as they spun together in their orbit round the sun at approximately one hundred and seven thousand, two hundred and fifty kilometres an hour –

almost three times faster than if he was travelling to the moon!

How extraordinary, he thought, that this same force of gravity, whose laws had been discovered by Newton, not only tied him to the earth and forced the moon to encircle the earth and the earth to revolve around the sun but also affected every single thing in the universe and even time and space itself, while thanks to Einstein, we now know that matter tells space-time how to curve and space-time tells matter how to move. But when did gravity begin?

Since man had landed on the moon, hundreds of space probes had orbited planets like Venus, Mars, Jupiter and Saturn and space craft like the two Voyager probes had even reached the outermost regions of the solar system. He reflected on the hundred thousand million stars in his own galaxy where other planets revolved round other suns and where stars like supernovas could blow themselves apart in explosions more destructive than any achieved by man.

The cosmic celebrity who once saw himself as a colossus astride his earth was now haunted by visions of a monster hurling rocks at his tiny planet until it whirled off its axis and reeled giddily into the vast emptiness of space.

....

XVII

DESOLATION

Mrs Faraday looked at the moon. It was huge and round and white with a filmy haze and glowed brighter than she had ever seen it before. But it was the black empty void that surrounded it which preoccupied her thoughts.

She imagined herself on the rim of a huge crater like a fly settling on its dead crust. She opened the window wide leaving her desolate thoughts to dissolve in the dusk. Like the image of her former soul-mate she would merge in its shadow.

It was three o'clock in the morning. Simon Faraday steered his new Honda motorbike by the light of the moon. He had smoked and his head was blurred with images.

The ghastly neon lights of town had trickled to

an end by a road junction and the moon had loomed in their place, huge and round like a massive white ball. It seemed to sink lower and lower in the sky so that any moment it might bounce and roll on to the earth.

All of a sudden a small vehicle swerved violently in front and forced the Honda on to a verge, tossing its rider head-first into a ditch.

Simon Faraday jerked his bike back on to the road. He could see a light shining from one of the rooms in the Mason's house which lay peacefully behind a row of sycamores and in the distance he caught sight of his own home, glinting beneath the moon, one of its windows opened wide to the cold night air.

Mary Faraday stood by the open window. The birds had stopped singing save for one which continued its shrill cry across the lawns of the neighbouring houses.

A car hooted in the silence and she saw the flash of a headlight beyond the row of sycamores near the Masons home. As the headlights faded, she could hear the sound of motorbike wheels over the tarmac road which became louder and louder until it finally stopped below her window. In the stark light of the moon she saw the blood-spattered face of her son.

Simon Faraday had grown aloof. He rarely spoke. His brother James was always so confident and wise that anything he himself tried to say appeared of little consequence. For this reason he resolved to become as non-committal as possible. This would at least endow him with an air of mystery whereas self-revelation only left him open to judgment and Simon Faraday could not bear to be judged. He smoked continually, balancing the cigarette on the edge of his lower lip or between the first two fingers of his right hand to give him a look of disdain and thereby conceal his sensitive, vulnerable nature.

At first he grew his hair long and wild. Then he cut it very short and dyed it different colours to match his clothes, changing his clothes to match his mood. When he felt particularly communicative he would wear his tattiest clothes which he adorned with loveable childhood figures. But more often he would disguise himself in stylish suits from the local jumble sales. His most formative role was as lead singer of Christopher Mason's group "The Mystics" when he spat into microphones and screamed when people were least expecting it. In this way he restored his old popularity with his friends who found his new image wildly exciting and his brother James rather a bore.

While each part of the Faraday household sought its own way of coping with their sudden tragic loss, Mrs Faraday was becoming increasingly alienated from her younger son. How could such a sensitive individual become so consumed by indifference and self-hatred?

She searched for ways to dispel his lethargy, remembering her husband's wise words:

"Do you realise that the earth has taken five thousand million years to evolve and that there are other suns and planets several tens of millions of light years from the sun?"

Simon Faraday raised his eyebrows and puffed at a cigarette so that smoke dangled in the air like a question mark.

"It took three thousand million years, dear, to produce people like us? Don't you realise that astronomy and physics and chemistry are based on the movements of the universe? What can you achieve by spitting into a microphone?"

Simon Faraday sighed deeply.

"That all the energy from the sun that gives us light – the very forces which synthesise the atoms of life – are still being used to create weapons of mass destruction?"

"Chaotic!" Simon Faraday agreed, puffing more smoke into the freshly aired room:

"Absolutely chaotic."

"It's your generation that must put things right, Simon. What will happen to your children and your children's children?"

"Hell!" agreed Simon Faraday, "Absolute Hell. Anyway, don't ask me, ask James."

....

XVIII

NEWS AT LAST

At exactly nineteen hours, the doorbell rang insistently, twice, three times. Mrs Faraday hurried to open it. It was the night she attended a course of lectures at the local adult education institute. Whoever could be disturbing her now?

To her surprise, the Masons were standing by the door, clearly anxious to talk to her.

"It's so amazing, amazing...!" began Mrs Mason breathlessly.

"Astonishing!" interjected her husband, "In the tropics of all places! Who could imagine such...?"

"You have no idea how excited we are!"

Like an automaton, Mrs Faraday moved to the television screen she had abandoned for months and the three took their places in front of it together with the two Faraday sons, as if taking part in the final act of a film.

"A lot of fog and drizzle," the grim voice of a news reader returned.

"But here to prove that no news is good news," a watery smile spread across his usually inscrutable face – good news was usually an anticlimax:

"No less than a miracle has brought our cosmic celebrity safely down to earth."

A picture of a haggard-looking man flashed on to the screen. His face was unshaven and deeply lined and his lustreless eyes appeared sunk into deep pits. Whoever had called Dr Faraday a God!

Mr Mason patted his wife's arm. He had to be up early. Every morning he went for an hour's run before travelling to his new office to prepare for the first guests for his new chain of motels.

His brain was firing on all cylinders. It was good to know his old friend was alive and well. Of course glory never lasted for ever. The ordeal had clearly taken its toll. Such a fit man! It might have served him better to have taken life a little less seriously. If only he had been more of a plodder like himself.

Yes, at this stage in life Mr Mason was at the peak of self-fulfilment supported by his solid wife. Even his children had become a source of great pride, though he feared that Christopher might fall under the negative influence of Simon Faraday.

"And let's hope that's an end to your troubles!" concluded Mr Mason with a benevolent smile at the screen.

"Yes", said Mrs Mason positively as they rose to leave, "Tomorrow is the start of a new lunar year – a time of rebirth and cosmic renewal."

....

XIX

CELEBRITY

No sooner had the Masons left than the phone began to ring again. Those who had abandoned Mrs Faraday at the moment of her tragic loss now returned to express their relief at her husband's miraculous survival. Hordes of journalists and photographers followed the trail of well-wishers to the Faraday home. What did Mrs Faraday feel now that her husband had been found?

Was she making any plans for the future?

The photographers eased their way into the house.

"Could Mrs Faraday stand just a little to the left? How did you feel when your husband disappeared?"

A sunshine home indeed! – The pool of gold at

the end of the rainbow. They snapped the sloping roofs and huge windows.

"Perhaps a picture of the living room?"

"Mrs Faraday in a reclining chair – a photo of the handsome man adoring the lovely wife at his side?"

"Could she just smile a little, though?"

"Think about your husband, Mrs Faraday!"

Mrs Faraday thought of her husband's worn, haggard face and anxiety creased its way across her forehead.

"And, maybe, yes, Mrs Faraday standing in the kitchen gazing across at the cedar tree?"

"And what about James Faraday? We heard he was quite a scientist like his father!"

James Faraday posed amongst his books on astronomy and physics.

"Perhaps a little frown – flick through some pages of Einstein," the photographers suggested. He flicked obligingly over the pages of a book by Albert Einstein:

"I shall never believe that God plays dice with the world," he read out slowly and frowned:

"I'm not sure about that!"

"And what about Simon Faraday? What has happened to him?"

Simon Faraday had changed into his most sober clothing, draped a trench-coat across his shoulders and donned a trilby in the style of Humphrey Bogart before creeping round the back of the house. Image makers were image breakers. A vulnerable, sensitive human being must protect himself.

He thundered up the tarmac drive on his Honda motorbike covering the photographers in an explosion of fumes as they snapped away regardless.

. . . .

XX

PAOLO SEES HIS GOD

A full moon shone over the house with the pambila roof where Paolo sat outside cross-legged and pensive. His vision had given him a new responsibility and he had to make his mind as clear as possible.

For this reason Paolo had eaten nothing except fish and bananas for five days. On the fifth day he swallowed some guayasu or herbal tea from a jungle vine which he had cooked over a small fire. Then he gulped down a drink of aniseed to take away the taste of the vine and lapsed into a trance.

His limbs dissolved like water, like clouds. His body melted into shadow. The sky and the stars, the delicate silhouette of the trees, the raucous chirping of the crickets and the chimes of the

forest were swallowed up into the black of the
night.

Paolo became smaller and smaller and the
sounds grew louder and louder and more and
more insistent. He sat quietly on the forest floor.
Hundreds of tiny suns were revolving in different
directions. They spun so fast that Paolo felt giddy.

He struggled to finish the juice of the herb. It
tasted sweet like honey. The sounds grew more
and more strident and raucous so every moment
it seemed as though a different bird or animal
was chirping or warbling.

Paolo started to whistle. He took a fan of
guanto leaves and shook them in the air so they
made a dry rustle while he lapsed into a deep
rhythmic song. Then he lit a cigar and started to
puff slowly so that narrow trails of smoke furled
above his head. The cigar smoothed his mind. He
began to see huge ships in the sky, curved like
canoes with long white sails that floated gently
over the clouds.

The next day Paolo and his wife Elena made
their way to a towering ceiba tree in the middle of
the forest.

The ceiba was so massive it towered above the
rest of the forest. Paolo called it the tree of
inspiration as it almost seemed to reach the

clouds. But Elena thought otherwise as it cast such large shadows that nothing could grow near it and only the wasps and the oriels built their nests in the topmost branches.

As Elena cut kapok from the ceiba bark to make quivers for their arrows, Paolo went to the river and clambered inside his small canoe. He thought of how he would build a new boat from the capirona tree and how they would later paint their youngest child with the red juice from the urubu berry for his first initiation ceremony.

Paolo looked at the sun and started to fish, letting the boat drift slowly along the narrow strip of river. For some time he sat peacefully as swallows swooped through the branches of the trees above him and woodpeckers chopped into their hollow barks with their long bills.

As he fished, Paolo heard a strange sound of droning through the sky which caused a flight of toucans to sweep past, flapping their wings in alarm and even the woodpeckers stopped their steady tap tapping against the trees.

He knew every sound in this corner of the world – the cry of the jaguar caught in a trap, the sudden crash of a tree as it fell to the ground, the sound of tapir hunting food or the wail of a monkey swinging from tree to tree – but this droning sound was something new.

Paolo sat in his canoe and looked up towards the sky. He could see an unusual shape like a large silver bird sailing over the trees. It dipped downwards in an arc and glided through the foliage before soaring upwards over the trees and into the clouds.

Paolo knew, of course, that this strange bird was carrying his God though he couldn't say whether it was flying to a house that shone like glass on the edge of the forest or to the end of a long long river that flowed on and on till the end of the world. It was a long way across the great mountains of the earth and Paolo knew that He was on his way to unite heaven and earth.

············

XXI

GOING HOME

A tiny helicopter dipped down from an azure sky and soared upwards like a huge bird.

As it swooped and swerved over the tops of the trees, the sides of the little aircraft shook so violently that its occupants could barely keep track of the muddy river below.

The helicopter made one final dip between two palms that rose majestically above the green forest and swooped down on to a narrow platform alongside the river where it shuddered to a halt.

Three men climbed out. One bent and haggard like an old man in odd white apparel, followed by a weary individual in an open-necked shirt and baggy trousers who scuffed the toes of his shoes against the wooden planks and finally, a small slight figure in faded blue jeans, silk shirt and old straw hat who moved swiftly as if triggered from a gun.

The three stood and waited as the small helicopter took off and soared back into the blue and another larger one swooped down in its place. Barely had the second landed than it too had vanished beyond the tree tops, bearing its three passengers to a small airport on the other side of the forest.

Crowds were swarming like ants on to the tarmac of the forest airport where the second helicopter landed. Officials sat on chairs by trestle tables, trying in vain to organise the mass of people which seemed to increase by the minute, while taxi drivers sat impatiently in their ancient cabs, touting for custom and hooting as luggage was dropped around them.

The passengers descended. First, the weary figure of Alberto, shuffling down the steps, followed by the spry gold prospector and finally the bent, haggard outline of Dr Faraday.

The crowd swarmed towards the plane while children pointed towards the stooped figure in his odd attire before he was whisked away with his spry companion in a large blue taxi.

For some time the taxi bumped over rough stony roads past wooden shacks and straw huts until it stopped outside a house with shuttered windows. Here the men were escorted up to a high-ceilinged room stacked with files and papers where a man sat typing slowly on an old Olivetti typewriter. He was young and wore glasses and he stared at the men in a not unfriendly way.

"Well, Felipe," Alberto made a helpless gesture with the palms of his hands.

"Here we are!" he sighed. It was very hot.

"Yes, Alberto. So I see!" said the man.

He stared at the haggard man in his torn white apparel and huge white boots.

There was no doubt about it. The man was mad.

He sighed too, very deeply, and then inhaled great gulps of air so his cheeks puffed out like a fish. Well, what was he to do? It was indeed very hot.

"Well, Alberto," he said at last. "I don't know."

They both sighed.

"You heard what happened recently to the Chief of Police?"

Alberto nodded.

"And the Governor of the State?"

"Even the Director of the University!"

They shook their heads.

Felipe turned to the haggard man.

"You have no papers?"

"No," replied Dr Faraday wearily. He had explained over and over again that he did not have papers.

"Well," said Felipe briskly. "Clearly we can't look after you here. You'll have to go."

He looked at a large clock on the wall, gathered up a handful of papers from his desk and banged them up and down a few times before going to open the door.

"Well, Adeus, Alberto," he shook Alberto's hand wearily.

"Adeus!" he nodded to the old man.

The men shuffled back into the large blue taxi which set off once more over the rough roads, past wooden shacks, back to the forest airport and the last stage of their journey together.

It just so happened that news of these latest events had filtered through to the next town which was the capital of this sleepy country.

Officials began to investigate which place on earth could possibly be responsible for such a mysterious being that appeared to have dropped down from the sky.

"It is just possible," declared one of the state department officials, "that this man came from the country Europa which recently sent a man to the moon. Following this event there was widespread alarm as the man mysteriously vanished and neither he nor his spacecraft were apparently seen again."

A picture of Dr Faraday was transmitted throughout the media. Telephones began to ring and officialdom forced to take immediate action. A representative from the country concerned was swiftly located who overcame such problems as lack of identity and money without more ado.

The celebrity astronaut was finally transported back to the land of his birth, his identity restored with no more than a simple piece of paper.

....

XXII

A FALLEN GOD

"**D**r Faraday!" cried the reporters as they swelled around him in the huge domed airport of his home country.

"How does it feel to be back on earth?"

"Can you tell us what happened to you?"

"What were your first impressions when you landed?"

"Can you recall some of your experiences?"

But Dr Faraday said nothing. No-one asked him why he was there and if they had he could not have answered.

Photographers forced their way through the crowds in an effort to recapture an image of the colossus who once whirled and spun around the globe on clouds of glory.

To their disappointment, instead of the

superman who posed so readily for their cameras, there was a dishevelled and confused individual who shielded his eyes from their gaze and had such difficulty walking that he had to be assisted by a member of the crew.

Only the shreds from his tattered white suit gave an indication of his former role as the twenty first century's first cosmic celebrity.

....

XXIII

THE WAY AHEAD

Mrs Mason was in deep meditation. She lit an incense candle and chanted quietly from memory:

"Shut out everything from without. See nothing. Hear nothing, and envelop your soul in absolute quiet and you will be carried to a land of great light – the source of positive power and through the gates of deep mystery, the source of negative power. These control Heaven and Earth, each is the other".

In this way Mrs Mason became one with the power that flowed through all things according to the wisdom of ancient Chinese philosophers who said: * "Listen with spirit...Spirit is empty and waits on all things."

* Chuang Tze "Mother of Pearls"

Nearby in the Faraday home, the television was silent. Mary Faraday sat with her two sons reading out loud from a small book:

"Look into space. You shall see Him walking in the cloud, outstretching His arm in the lightning and descending in rain. You shall see Him smiling in flowers and waving His hand in trees."

Then she turned over a page she had carefully marked and read:

"And an astronomer said: * "Master what of Time?"

And he answered:

"And that which sings and contemplates in you is still dwelling within the bounds of that first moment which scattered the stars into space."

* Khalil Gibran "The Prophet"

Fergus Faraday stared at the cedar outside his solar home. It looked so solid he wondered how old it was – three times older than him at least. He looked at the grass that stretched around the tree and marvelled how green and lush it seemed. He sat gazing at the sky through the windows of his home and let time drift by.

He tried to share his experiences with his wife but whenever he tried to focus on their past some other time and space would intrude. His thoughts would shift from one dimension to the next and he would shut his eyes as if space was squeezing him more and more till he became no more than a tiny strand of energy, more insignificant than even the most remote atom in the universe.

....